For the journey home.

Purple Little Bird

By Greg Foley

BALZER + BRAY
An Imprint of HarperCollinsPublishers

Purple Little Bird loved everything purple.
He lived in a purple little house with a purple little fence
and a very purple garden.

Purple Little Bird worked hard to make his house perfect.

But no matter what he did,

something was not quite right.

So one day, he packed a bag

and went looking for a truly perfect place.

Purple Little Bird walked all the way
to Brown Bear's cave.

"I'm looking for the perfect place," he said.
"My cave is warm and cozy," said Brown Bear.

"It is warm and cozy," said Purple Little Bird.
"But it's too dark!"

So Purple Little Bird climbed a steep cliff to see Gray Goat.
"I'm looking for the perfect place," he said.

"It's bright and sunny here," said Gray Goat.
"It is bright and sunny," said Purple Little Bird. "But . . .

it's too windy!"

Purple Little Bird continued on until he met Yellow Camel.
"Maybe this is the perfect place," he said.

"My desert is nice and quiet," said Yellow Camel.
"It is nice and quiet," said Purple Little Bird. "But . . .

it's too dusty!"

Then Purple Little Bird found Blue Frog in his pond.
"I hope this is the perfect place," he said.

"My pond is very cool and refreshing," said Blue Frog.
"It is cool and refreshing," said Purple Little Bird. "But …

it's too damp!"

So Purple Little Bird kept going
until he saw a beautiful tree.

Three Pink Possums hung there in a row.

He told the Pink Possums all the places he'd been.
"We know a place," they said, "that isn't too dark,
windy, dusty, or damp."

So Purple Little Bird followed the Possums.

To his surprise, they stopped at a purple little house
with a purple little fence and a very purple garden.

Purple Little Bird looked around.
"You know what's wrong with this place?" he said.

"It's much too purple!

But now I know what to do."

So they made it perfect.

Balzer + Bray is an imprint of HarperCollins Publishers.

Purple Little Bird   Copyright © 2011 by Greg Foley   All rights reserved.   Manufactured in China.
For information address HarperCollins Children's Books, a division of HarperCollins Publishers, 10 East 53rd Street, New York, NY 10022.   www.harpercollinschildrens.com
Library of Congress Cataloging-in-Publication Data is available.   ISBN 978-0-06-200828-2
11 12 13 14 15   SCP   10 9 8 7 6 5 4 3 2 1   ❖   First Edition